D0604473

A TREASURY OF SIX ORIGINAL STORIES

Good Night, Baby Animals
You've Had a Busy Day

KAREN B. WINNICK   illustrated by LAURA WATKINS

HENRY HOLT • NEW YORK

Tiger Babies Romp

When Mama goes out to hunt,
tiger babies creep away
from their den.

Tiger noses **sniff.**
Tiger ears **twitch, twitch.**
Tiger tails **swish, swish, swish.**
What's moving?

A SNAKE!

Tiger babies dash
through the tall grass.
Dash, dash, dash to . . .

A TREE!
Up, up, up tiger babies climb.
Tiger noses **sniff**.
Tiger ears **twitch, twitch**.
Tiger tails **swish, swish, swish**.
What's over there?

Tiger babies jump
down, down, down.
They **dash** through
the tall grass.
Dash, dash, dash to . . .

A LAKE!

SPLASH   SPLASH
     SPLASH

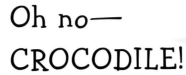

Oh no—
CROCODILE!

SPLASH
SPLASH
SPLASH

Tiger babies **run**
through the tall grass.
Run, run, run . . .

. . . to their den!
Tiger babies rumble.
Rumble, tumble, tumble.
A JUMBLE!

Mama comes back with meat.
Tiger babies **eat, eat, eat**.
Then tiger babies **sleep**.

*Good night, baby tigers—
you've had a busy day.*

Baby Elephant's Little Trunk

When baby elephants are born,
they don't know how to use their trunk.
So . . .

Baby Elephant watches Mama.

Sniff, sniff.
Mama whiffs the
air with her trunk.

Sniff, sniff.
Baby Elephant whiffs, too!

Rub, rub.
Mama rubs her head,
her ear, her knee.

Rub, rub.
Baby Elephant rubs
his head, his ear,
his knee, too!

Up, up.
Mama reaches leaves.

Up, up.
Baby Elephant almost
reaches leaves!

Down, down.
Mama grabs clumps of grass.
She picks up tiny seeds.

Down, down.
Baby Elephant does, too!

Munch, munch.
Munch! Munch!

Poof, poof.
Mama shoos bugs.
Poof, poof.
Baby Elephant shoos, too!

Baby Elephant
follows Mama . . .

to the water hole.
Mama scoops water.
Baby Elephant scoops, too.
SPLASH!
SPLATTER!
SPLAT!

Mama rumbles.
Baby Elephant runs to her side.
With his trunk, he hugs Mama.

Good night, Baby Elephant—
you've had a busy day.

Is Baby Giraffe Tall Enough?

Baby Giraffe is just born.
She push, pushes
on her spindly new legs.
She stands!

Baby Giraffe takes her
first step: **wobble**!
Then another
wobble, wobble.

Baby Giraffe is walking!

She stops and watches
the older, taller calves.
They stretch their long legs
and nibble leaves.

So Baby Giraffe stretches
her legs **up**, **up** and almost
reaches a leaf.
Not tall enough yet.

The other calves thrust out their long necks and chomp branches.

So Baby Giraffe thrusts out her neck **up**, **up** and almost grabs a branch.
Not tall enough yet.

The calves curl their long tongues up and crunch seed pods.

So Baby Giraffe curls her tongue **up**, **up** and almost pulls off a pod. *Not tall enough yet.*

Baby Giraffe runs to Mama's side.

She stretches her legs **up**, **up**.
She thrusts her neck **up**, **up**.
She curls her tongue **up**, **up**.
Baby Giraffe is just born,
yet she is tall enough to . . .

. . . glub, glub
Mama's milk.

Glub, glub, glub.
Baby Giraffe's belly is full.

Safe beneath Mama,
she folds her spindly legs.

*Good night, Baby Giraffe—
you've had a busy day.*

Brave Baby Rhino

Baby Rhino trots with Mama.
He stops.
He turns his head left.
He blinks.
He turns his head right.
He squints.
Could that be a lion?

Baby Rhino paws
the ground.
CHARGE!
No lion—just a
big rock.

Mama snorts.
Baby Rhino gallops
with Mama.
He stops.

He turns his head left.

He blinks.

He turns his head right.
He squints.
Could that be a leopard?

Baby Rhino flattens his ears.
CHARGE!
No leopard—just a tree stump.

Mama snorts.
Baby Rhino tramps
along with Mama.
He stops.

He turns his head left.

He blinks.

He turns his head right.
He squints.
Could that be a crocodile?

No crocodile . . .

. . . just a mound of mud!
The mud is warm. The mud is soft.
Baby Rhino and Mama **roll, roll, roll**!
Together they **snort, snort, snort**!

Soon Baby Rhino and Mama
snore, snore, snore.

*Good night, Baby Rhino—
you've had a busy day.*

Hungry, Hungry Panda

Baby Panda blinks.
He yawns and stretches.
His stomach rumbles.
But Mama snores and snores.
He scurries away to find . . .

bamboo!
Baby Panda **cracks** the
stalks above their roots.
He **snaps** the stems
and **chomps** the shoots.

And then he sleeps.
Baby Panda wakes.
Where's Mama?

He pads over pine needles and branches.
A stream!
A round white face with black patches
stares back.
Is that Mama?

Baby Panda touches the water.
The face is gone!

Baby Panda's
stomach rumbles.
Up the mountain
he trudges to find . . .

. . . bamboo!
Baby Panda **cracks** the
stalks above their roots.
He **snaps** the stems
and **chomps** the shoots.
And then he sleeps.

Baby Panda wakes.
Where could Mama be?
Baby Panda grabs a long
vine with his teeth.
He twists. He turns.
He twirls around and around.
Baby Panda is trapped!
He **roars** and **roars**.
HELP!

A round white face
with black patches
appears.
Mama pulls
Baby Panda free.

He tumbles and topples.
He flips and flops.
He **yips** and **yaps** and **yips**.

Then Baby Panda's
stomach rumbles.
Mama's rumbles, too.
They trot off to find . . .

. . . bamboo!
Baby Panda and Mama **crack**
the stalks above their roots.
They **snap** the stems
and **chomp** the shoots.
And then . . . they sleep!

Good night, Baby Panda—
you've had a busy day.

Time to Play, Baby Gorilla!

Up, up the mountain,
Baby Gorilla, Mama, aunts, and cousins
follow Papa to find food.
Baby Gorilla rides on Mama's back.
But Baby Gorilla wants to play.

She jumps
to the ground.

Mama catches
Baby Gorilla and
holds her tight.

Up, up Papa leads the
troop through the wet forest.
But Baby Gorilla
wants to play.

She scoots
to a branch.

Mama pulls her down
and lifts Baby Gorilla
onto her back.

Up, **up** the troop tramps over big rocks.

Papa beats his chest.
He's found celery stalks!
Bamboo shoots! Fruit!

Papa rips stalks. Mama, aunts, and cousins chomp shoots.

But Baby Gorilla wants to play. She zooms around trees.

Mama grabs Baby Gorilla.
She feeds her fruit.

Papa rests under a tree.
Mama, aunts, and cousins
rest in the grass.
Mama pats Baby Gorilla.

Now it is time to play.
But Baby Gorilla shuts
her eyes.

*Good night, Baby Gorilla—
you've had a busy day.*

ANIMAL

Tiger

Tigers are the biggest cats in the world. They live in different parts of Asia. Each tiger has a unique pattern of stripes. Tiger cubs are born blind and live on their mother's milk until they are ready to eat meat. Cubs love to chase and wrestle with each other.

Elephant

African elephants are the largest land animals. They eat leaves and bark from trees, grasses, and shrubs. Sometimes they can eat as much as six hundred pounds of food in one day! Elephants live in family groups. The oldest female is the leader. She shows the others where to find water and watches out for danger.

Giraffe

Giraffes live in Africa and are the tallest animals. They munch leaves most other animals can't reach. One mother stays with all the babies when the other mothers in the herd go off to eat. Giraffes protect themselves and their babies against other animals with powerful kicks.

FACTS

Rhinoceros

Rhinos are the second-biggest land animal after elephants. Some live in Africa, others in Asia. They graze on grass or eat leaves from trees and bushes. Rhinos smell and hear well, but their eyesight is poor. They roll in mud to protect their skin from sun and bugs. Rhino babies stay close by their mothers. Mothers will charge a lion to protect their calves.

Panda

Pandas live in the mountainous forests of China. They spend at least twelve hours a day eating bamboo. When a baby panda is born, it is tiny and pink and has no hair. The mother panda gently cradles her baby with one paw. She holds it close to her body.

Gorilla

Mountain gorillas live in the forests of central Africa within family groups called troops. A male gorilla leads his troop when they look for food. A baby travels with its mother, riding on her back or clinging to her belly. Each night, gorillas build a nest of leaves on the ground or in low trees, where they sleep and snuggle with their young.

To Sophia, Jacob, Wesley, Myla, Benny,
Sara, and Teddy with love
—K.B.W.

For my dad and all his stories
—L.W.

Henry Holt and Company, *Publishers since 1866*
175 Fifth Avenue, New York, New York 10010
mackids.com

Henry Holt® is a registered trademark of Macmillan Publishing Group, LLC.

Library of Congress Cataloging-in-Publication Data
Names: Winnick, Karen B., author. | Watkins, Laura, illustrator.
Title: Good night, baby animals you've had a busy day : a treasury of six original stories /
Karen B. Winnick ; illustrated by Laura Watkins.
Description: First edition. | New York : Henry Holt and Company, 2017.
Summary: "Six read-aloud stories for toddlers about baby animals in the wild:
tiger, elephant, giraffe, rhinoceros, panda, and gorilla" —Provided by publisher.
Identifiers: LCCN 2016007335 | ISBN 9780805098839 (hardback)
Subjects: LCSH: Jungle animals—Juvenile fiction. | Children's stories, American.
CYAC: Jungle animals—Fiction. | Animals—Infancy—Fiction. | Short stories.
BISAC: JUVENILE FICTION / Animals / General. | JUVENILE FICTION / Bedtime & Dreams.
Classification: LCC PZ10.3.W6855 Go 2017 | DDC [E]—dc23
LC record available at https://lccn.loc.gov/2016007335

Our books may be purchased in bulk for promotional, educational, or business use. Please contact your local
bookseller or the Macmillan Corporate and Premium Sales Department at (800) 221-7945 ext. 5442 or by e-mail
at MacmillanSpecialMarkets@macmillan.com.

First edition—2017 / Designed by Eileen Savage
The artist used mixed media, including pencil, acrylics, and watercolors,
digitally enhanced, to create the illustrations for this book.
Printed in China by Toppan Leefung Printing Ltd., Dongguan City, Guangdong Province

1   3   5   7   9   10   8   6   4   2